W9-AHJ-325

Juvenile

SCHAUMBURG TOWNSHIP DISTRICT LIBRARY

3 1257 01724 0721

WITHDRAWN

HANOVER PARK BRANCH

Schaumburg Township District Library

130 South Roselle Road

Schaumburg, Illinois 60193

I'm Going To READ!™

These levels are meant only as guides;
you and your child can best choose a book that's right.

Level 1: Kindergarten–Grade 1 . . . Ages 4–6

- word bank to highlight new words
- consistent placement of text to promote readability
- easy words and phrases
- simple sentences build to make simple stories
- art and design help new readers decode text

Level 2: Grade 1 . . . Ages 6–7

- word bank to highlight new words
- rhyming texts introduced
- more difficult words, but vocabulary is still limited
- longer sentences and longer stories
- designed for easy readability

Level 3: Grade 2 . . . Ages 7–8

- richer vocabulary of up to 200 different words
- varied sentence structure
- high-interest stories with longer plots
- designed to promote independent reading

Level 4: Grades 3 and up . . . Ages 8 and up

- richer vocabulary of more than 300 different words
- short chapters, multiple stories, or poems
- more complex plots for the newly independent reader
- emphasis on reading for meaning

LEVEL 3

Library of Congress Cataloging-in-Publication Data Available

2 4 6 8 10 9 7 5 3

Published by Sterling Publishing Co., Inc.
387 Park Avenue South, New York, NY 10016
Text © 2005 by Harriet Ziefert Inc.
Illustrations © 2005 by Andrea Baruffi
Distributed in Canada by Sterling Publishing
c/o Canadian Manda Group, 165 Dufferin Street,
Toronto, Ontario, Canada M6K 3H6
Distributed in the United Kingdom by GMC Distribution Services,
Castle Place, 166 High Street, Lewes, East Sussex, England BN7 1XU
Distributed in Australia by Capricorn Link (Australia) Pty. Ltd.
P.O. Box 704, Windsor, NSW 2756, Australia

I'm Going To Read is a trademark of Sterling Publishing Co., Inc.

Printed in China
All rights reserved

Sterling ISBN-13: 978-1-4027-3027-6
ISBN-10: 1-4027-3027-6

For information about custom editions, special sales, premium and
corporate purchases, please contact Sterling Special Sales
Department at 800-805-5489 or specialsales@sterlingpub.com.

I'm Going To
READ!™

IF I HAD
A ROBOT DOG

Pictures by Andrea Baruffi

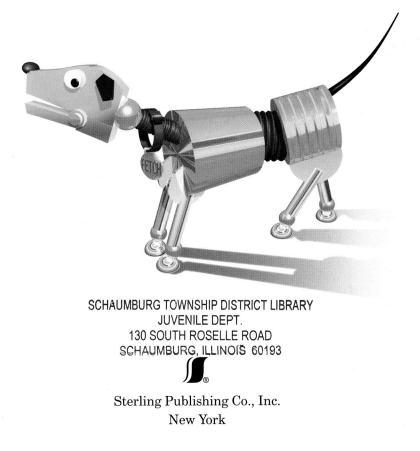

SCHAUMBURG TOWNSHIP DISTRICT LIBRARY
JUVENILE DEPT.
130 SOUTH ROSELLE ROAD
SCHAUMBURG, ILLINOIS 60193

Sterling Publishing Co., Inc.
New York

3/06
Penn
$14 —

READER
ZIEFERT, H

3 1257 01724 0721

CHAPTER 1

FETCH

If I had a robot dog,
Sometimes we could play.
But if I wanted something,
This is what I'd say:

Fetch my CD's
and my boom box!

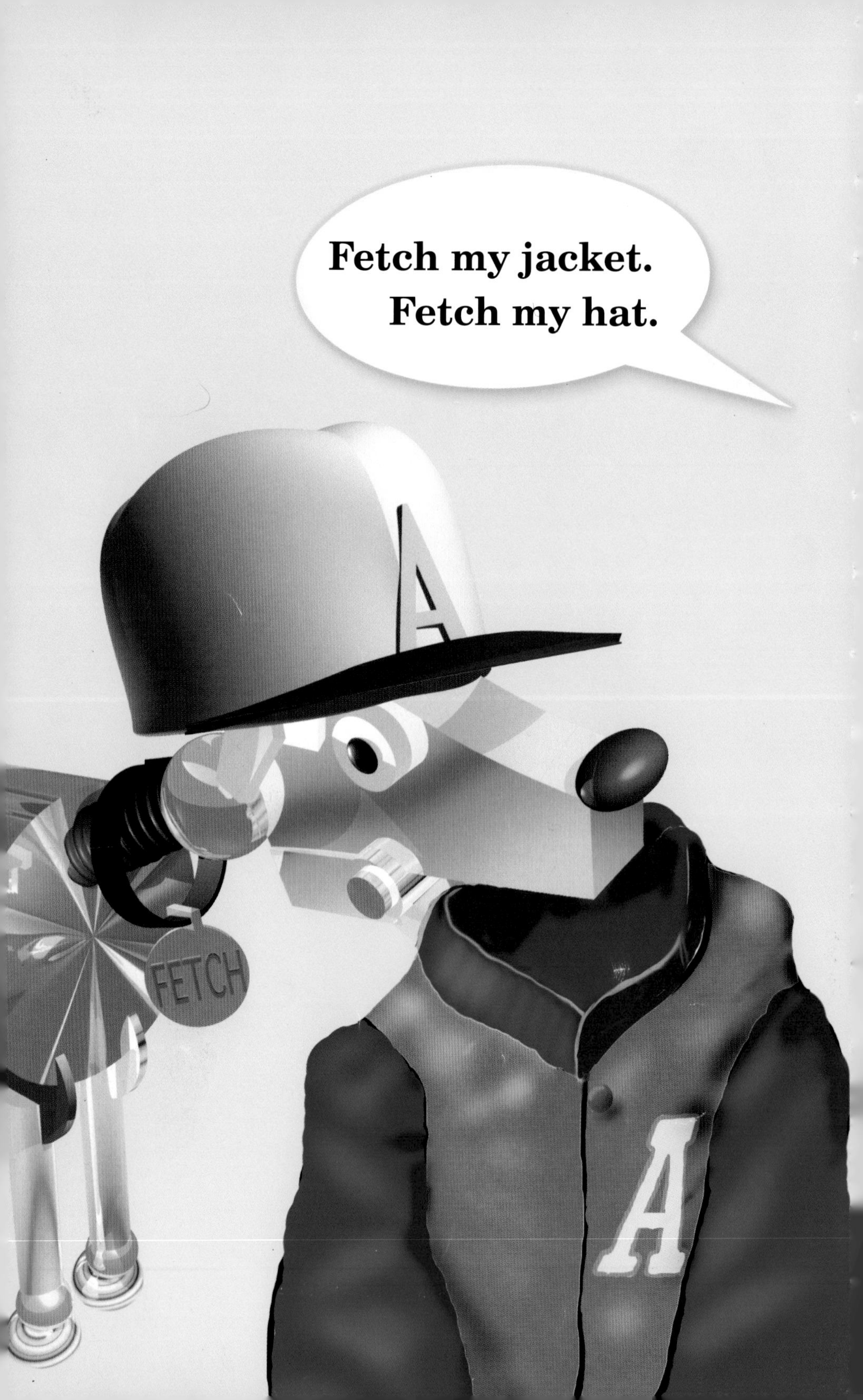
Fetch my jacket.
Fetch my hat.
FETCH

Fetch my ball
and my good bat.

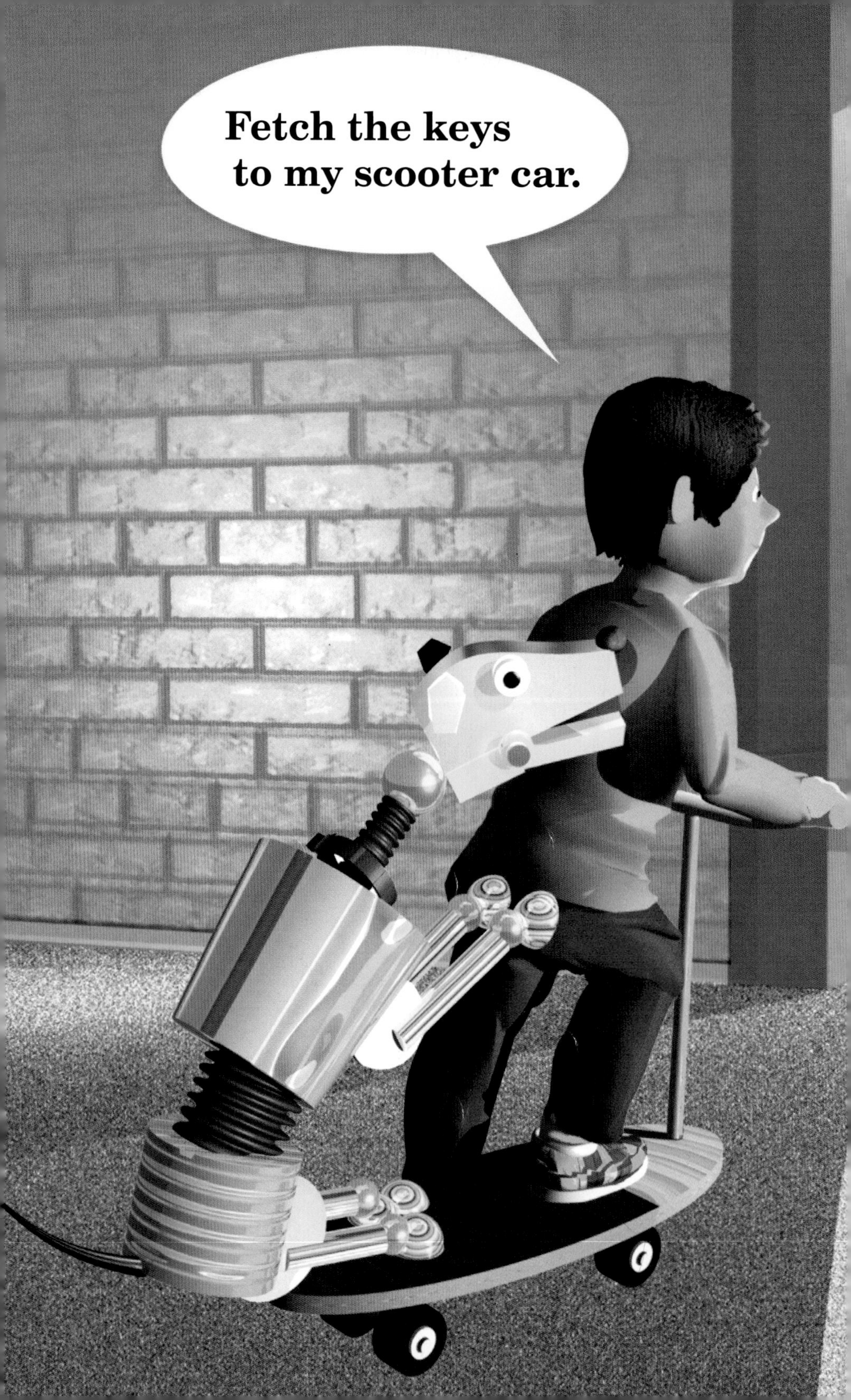
Fetch the keys to my scooter car.

I'll give you a ride,
but not too far.

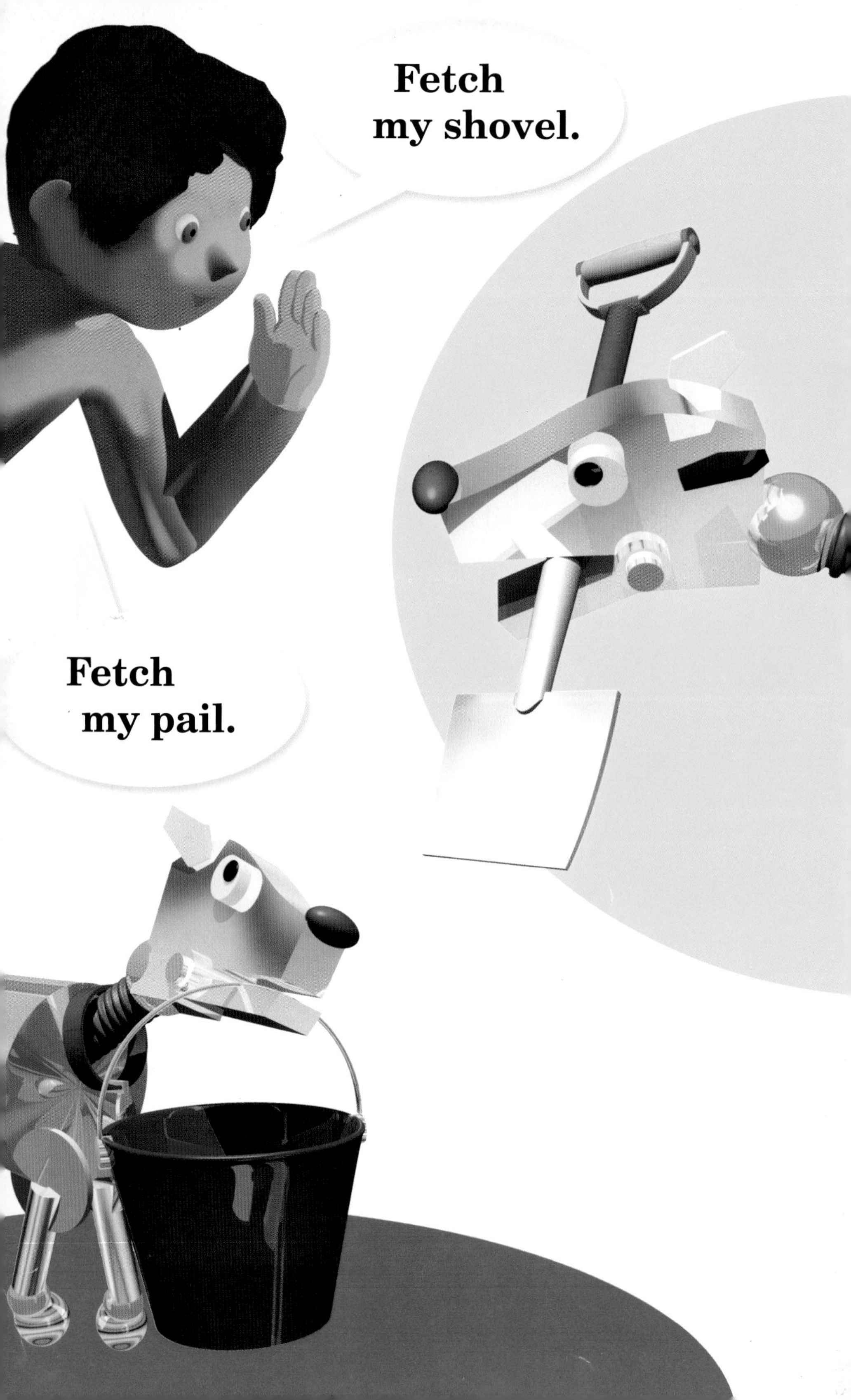
Fetch my shovel.
Fetch my pail.

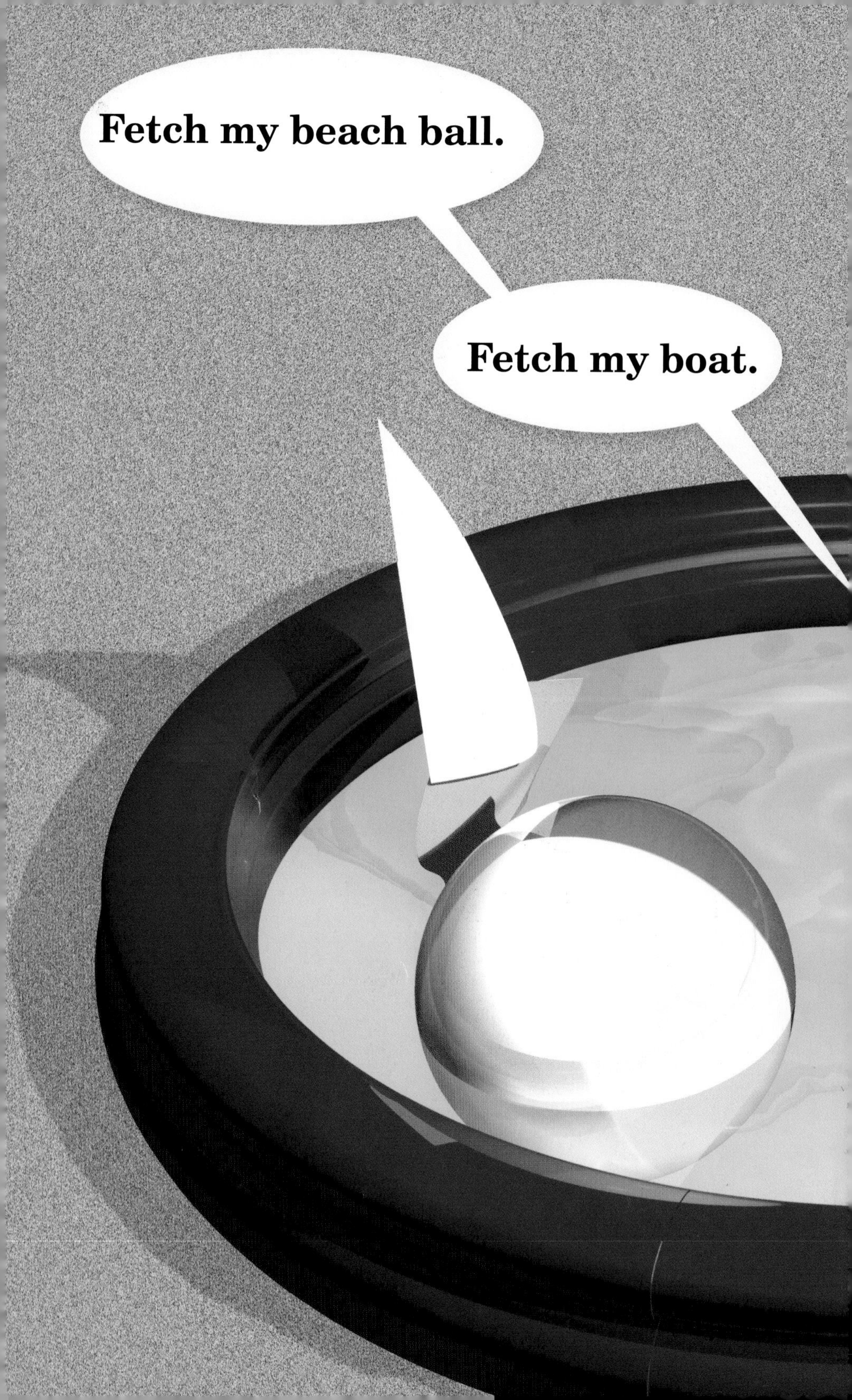
Fetch my beach ball.
Fetch my boat.

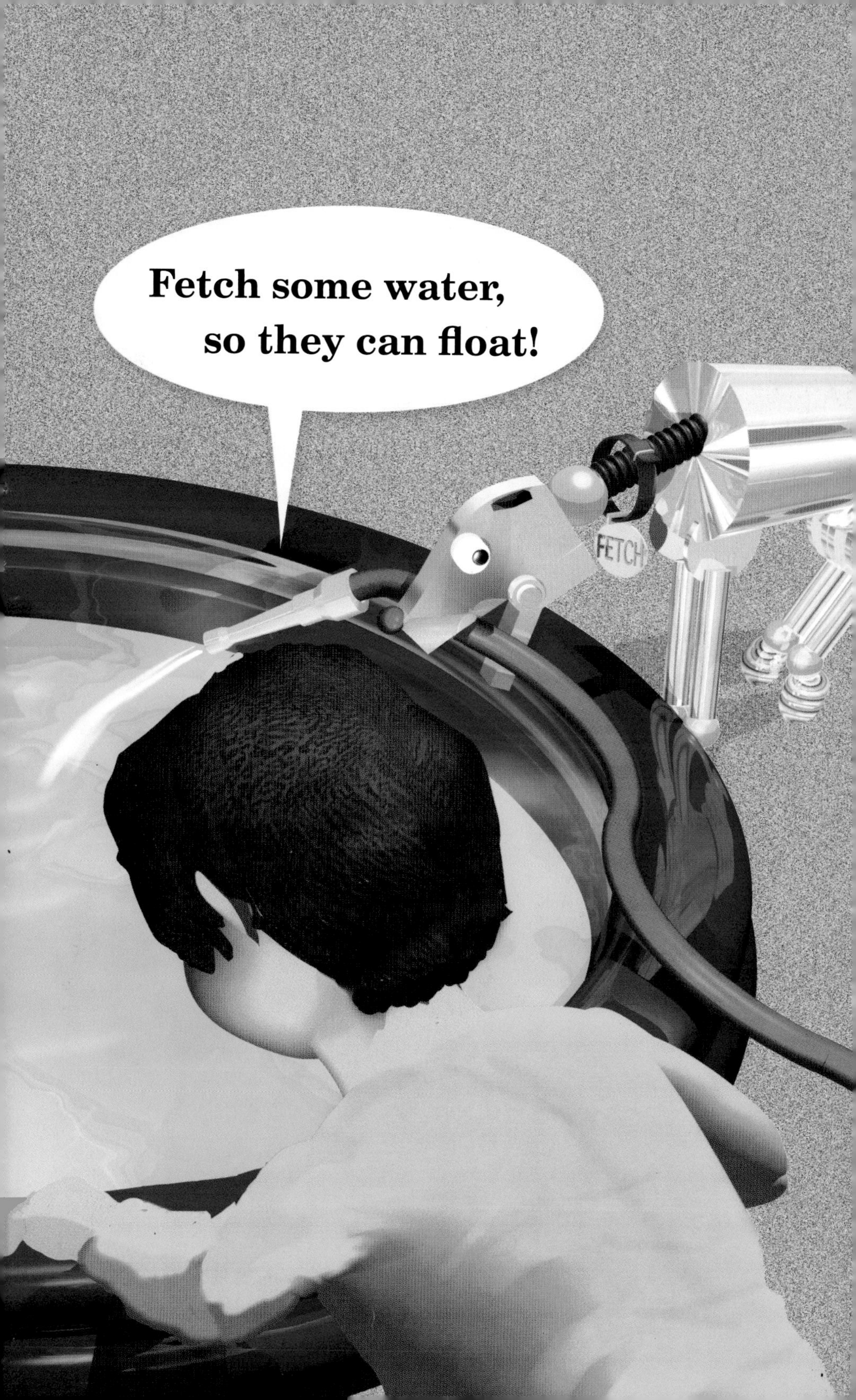
Fetch some water, so they can float!
FETCH

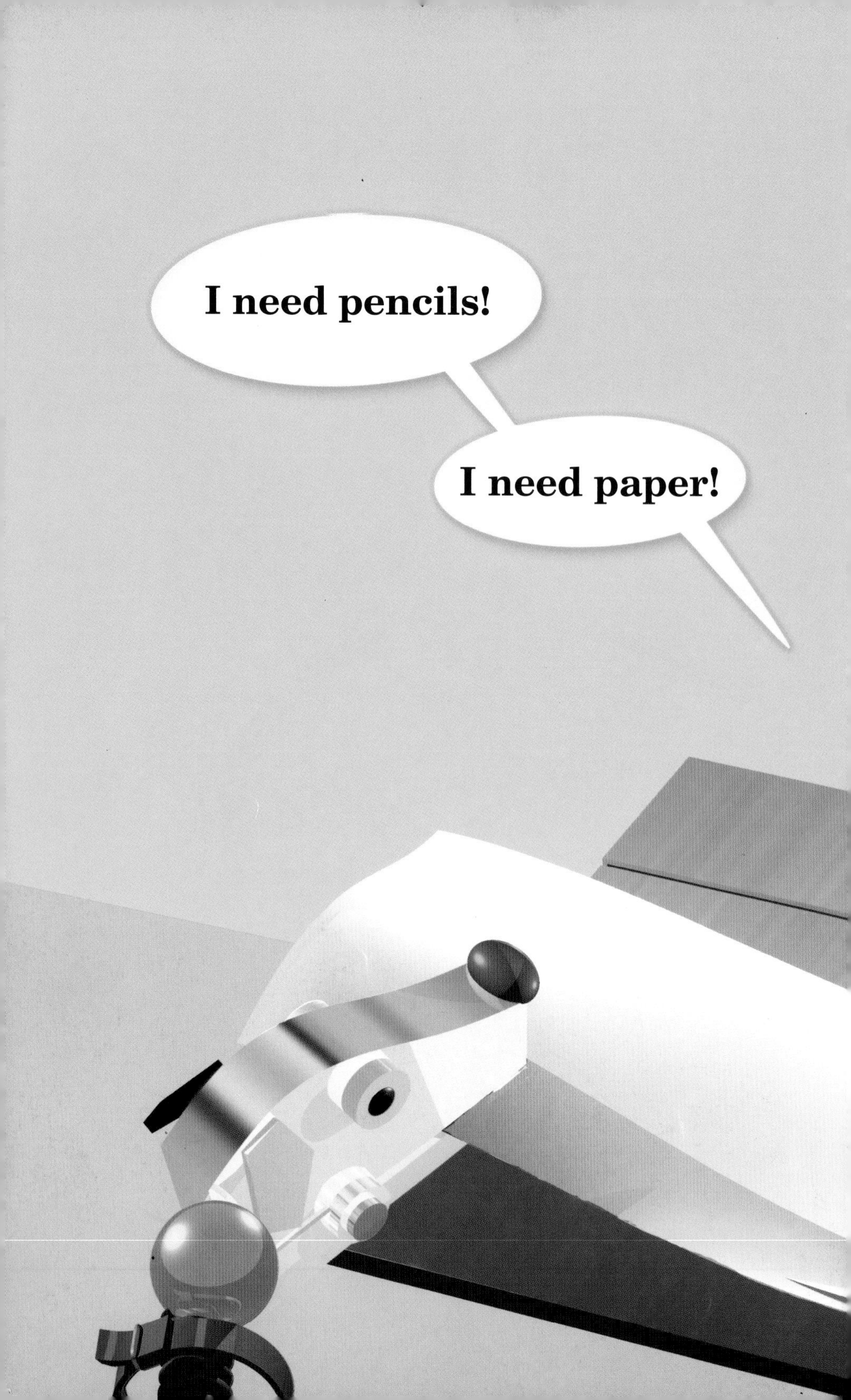
I need pencils!
I need paper!

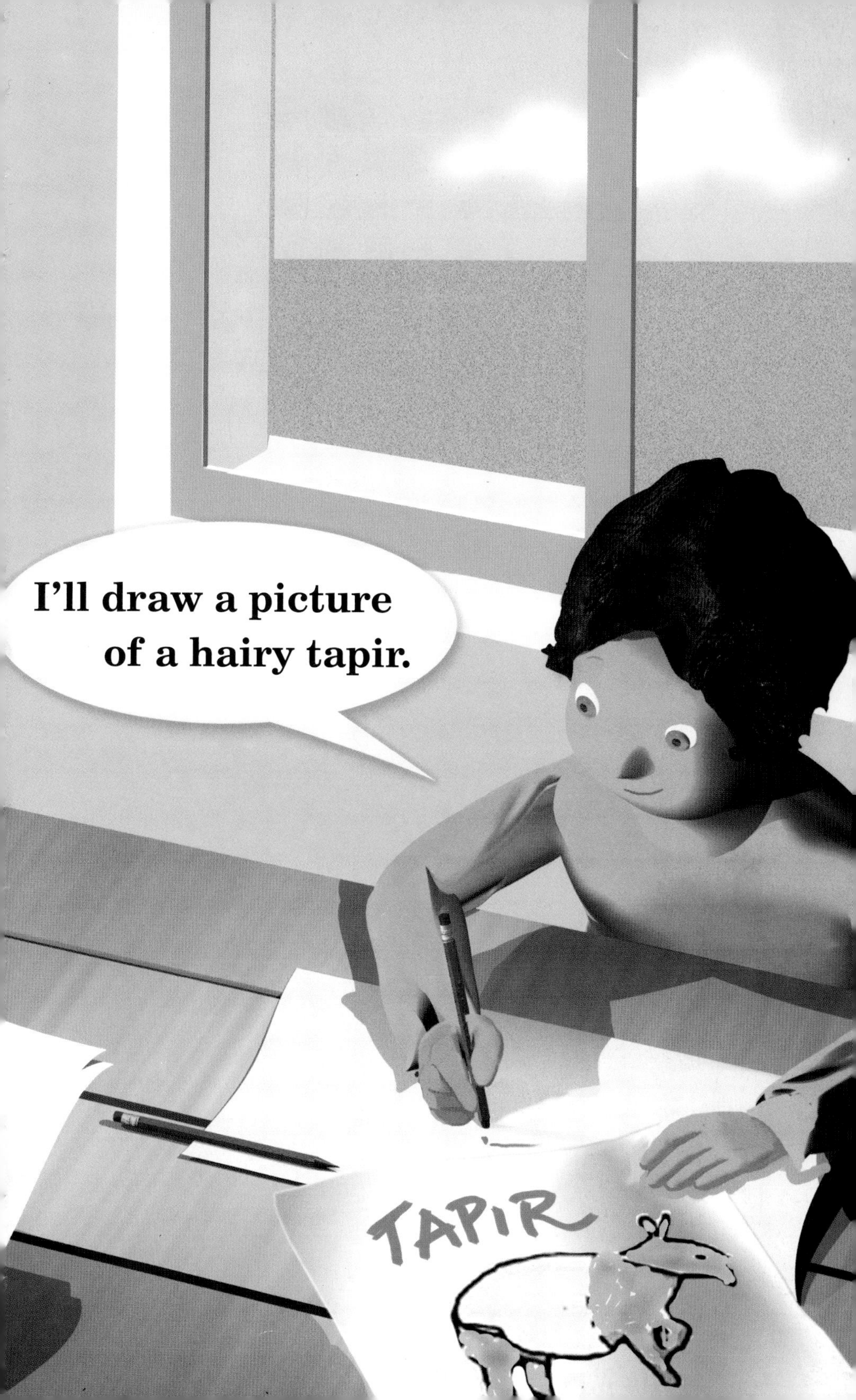
I'll draw a picture of a hairy tapir.
TAPIR

You did enough fetching for one day. Thank you, Doggie, here's your pay!

CHAPTER 2

IN THE PARK

It's nice to have a robot
To walk me to the park.
It's nice to have a robot
Who doesn't ever bark.

I want a turn
on the merry-go-round.
Please stop it, Robot,
from going around.

Robot Doggie, push my swing.
Get me higher than anything!

Scare the black dog
over there.
She looks as mean
as a grizzly bear.

Robot, Robot,
run after me.
I need someone
to race me to the tree.

Now your power
is getting low.
I'll charge your battery,
so you can go!